THE BABY-SITTERS CLUB

DAWN AND THE IMPOSSIBLE THREE

DON'T MISS THE OTHER
BABY-SITTERS CLUB GRAPHIC NOVELS!

ANN M. MARTIN

THE BABY-SITTERS CLUB®

DAWN AND THE IMPOSSIBLE THREE

A GRAPHIC NOVEL BY

GALE GALLIGAN

WITH COLOR BY BRADEN LAMB

graphix

An Imprint of

■SCHOLASTIC

Library of Congress Control Number: 2016960080

ISBN 978-1-338-06730-9 (hardcover)
ISBN 978-1-338-06711-8 (paperback)

10   20 21

Printed in Malaysia   108
First edition, October 2017

Edited by Cassandra Pelham and David Levithan
Book design by Phil Falco
Creative Director: David Saylor

For Aunt Dot
A. M. M.

Eternal thanks to Mom, Dad, Lori, A. M. M.,
Raina Telgemeier, Cassandra Pelham, David Saylor,
David Levithan, Phil Falco, Sheila Marie Everett, Braden Lamb,
John Green, Dave Roman, Rachel Young, Ngozi Ukazu,
Dave Valeza, and all my beloved friends,
family, and grads.

And to Patrick, who gets his very own line
because he is my favorite boy.
G. G.

KRISTY THOMAS
PRESIDENT

CLAUDIA KISHI
VICE PRESIDENT

DAWN SCHAFER
ALTERNATE OFFICER

MARY ANNE SPIER
SECRETARY

STACEY MCGILL
TREASURER

CHAPTER 1

I'M STILL NOT SURE WHAT THE BIG DEAL ABOUT NEW ENGLAND WINTERS IS.

I'VE ONLY LIVED HERE A FEW MONTHS.

LAST FALL MY PARENTS SPLIT UP, AND MOM DECIDED TO UPROOT US FROM SUNNY CALIFORNIA...

huff puff

tk tk tk

TO FREEZING CONNECTICUT.

dinga ling

I'LL GET IT! I'LL GET IT!

HI, CLAIRE!

MY NAME IS DAWN SCHAFER, AND I'M THE NEWEST MEMBER OF THE BABY-SITTERS CLUB.

OR, WELL, I WAS.

WHAT'S EIGHT TIMES SEVEN?

HI, MAL. YOU KNOW THAT ONE.

THIS IS MALLORY.

...

FIFTY-SIX?

SHE'S HELPED US BABY-SIT BEFORE.

RIGHT!

THANKS! THAT'S ALL I HAD LEFT.

SNACK TIME??

SURE.

whoosh

IN FACT, TODAY WILL BE HER FIRST DAY AS AN OFFICIAL JUNIOR MEMBER OF THE BSC.

7

15

ONLY ONE EARRING

RUBBER BAND

PRICE TAG

MOM, FOR HEAVEN'S SAKE.

WHAT WOULD I DO WITHOUT YOU, DAWN?

snap

MUCH BETTER. AND I'M OFF!

ALL RIGHT, SAY HI TO MR. SPIER FOR --

. . .

EARRING!

UUUUGH.

glorp

LEFTOVER STEW.

C'MON, C'MON.

PIZZA

HEY, JEFF!

ORGANIC FROZEN PIZZA?

YES, **PLEASE.**

ding!

ring
rin

ring ring

BOOOOO.

25

HELLO?

DAWN! IT'S MARY ANNE. WHAT ARE YOU UP TO?

nom

EATING DINNER.

OH! I SHOULD'VE ASKED YOU OVER SO YOU WOULDN'T HAVE TO EAT ALONE.

THAT'S OKAY.

LISTEN, I HAVE A GREAT IDEA.

snarf

DO YOU WANT TO HELP ME REDO MY ROOM?

YEAH!

YOU KNOW WHAT? WE HAVE A TON OF SPARE STUFF THAT I BET YOU'D LOVE.

POSTERS, PICTURE FRAMES, A CUTE LAMP...

I DON'T KNOW... DOESN'T YOUR MOM WANT THOSE THINGS?

NAH.

WE WERE GOING TO HAVE A GARAGE SALE BUT NEVER GOT AROUND TO IT.

WELL...

WHY DON'T I COME OVER TOMORROW AND BRING SOME STUFF WITH ME?

IF YOU LIKE IT, IT'S YOURS. IF NOT, WE'LL THINK OF OTHER THINGS TO DO TO YOUR ROOM.

OKAY!

noogie

THE NEXT DAY, I WENT THROUGH THE ATTIC AND FOUND SO MUCH STUFF THAT MOM HAD TO DRIVE ME OVER TO THE SPIERS'.

THIS WAS A LITTLE SNEAKY ON MY PART, SINCE IT SERVED THREE PURPOSES.

ONE, I GOT A RIDE...

TWO, WHEN MARY ANNE SAW MY MOM, SHE'D KNOW IT WAS OKAY TO USE OUR THINGS...

I'D LOVE TO SEE THESE GO TO GOOD USE.

THANKS A LOT, MRS. SCHAFER. THIS IS SO NICE OF YOU.

AND THREE, IT WOULD GIVE US A CHANCE TO SEE HOW THE BIG DATE WENT.

OH! SHARON! GOODNESS, LET ME HELP YOU WITH THAT.

YOU'RE MAKING ME LOOK BAD! AT LEAST PRETEND IT WEIGHS **SOMETHING.**

LUGGING AROUND PAPERWORK ALL DAY **DOES** HAVE ITS BENEFITS.

hee hee

hee hee

HI. WHAT'S ALL THIS STUFF?

DAWN BROUGHT IT OVER.

DAD'S LETTING ME TAKE THE OLD STUFF OFF MY WALLS AND PUT UP WHATEVER I WANT!

HE'S LETTING YOU PUT **THUMBTACKS** IN THE **WALLS?**

I GUESS SO.

HOW COME YOU DIDN'T TELL **ME** YOU WERE GOING TO START REDECORATING?

I DON'T KNOW...

HEY, DID I TELL YOU? OUR PARENTS WENT ON ANOTHER DATE LAST NIGHT... A **SPONTANEOUS** ONE.

OH...THAT'S COOL, I GUESS.

YOU KNOW...

29

THIS PLACE WAS A MESS!!

DAWN? DAWN, IS THAT YOU?

HI, MRS. BARRETT.

WHERE DO YOU KEEP YOUR—

SO LONG, DARLINGS. BE GOOD FOR DAWN.

WAIT! WHERE ARE YOU GOING TO BE?

AT A JOB INTERVIEW. AND I'M LATE.

WHAT IF THERE'S AN EMERGENCY? HOW DO I REACH YOU?

CALL THE PIKES, OKAY?

WELL...

ALL RIGHT.

SCREEEEEEE

USUALLY, I GET SOME KIND OF SPECIAL INSTRUCTION.

SNACK TIME AT 4, NO TV BEFORE HOMEWORK...

UH...

SOMETHING.

YOU GUYS EVER SEE *MARY POPPINS*?

NOPE.

WELL...HOW WOULD YOU LIKE TO PLAY A GAME?

YEAH!!

38

THIS SURE IS NICER, ISN'T IT?

YEAH!

EVEN THOUGH WE DIDN'T BEAT THE RECORD THIS TIME.

HEY, DAWN?

YEAH?

DO YOU HAVE A DADDY?

WELL...YES. BUT NOT HERE. HE DOESN'T LIVE WITH US.

YEAH. HE'S IN CALIFORNIA. THREE THOUSAND MILES AWAY.

REALLY?

MY MOM AND DAD ARE DIVORCED.

SO ARE OURS.

BY THE TIME MRS. BARRETT CAME BACK...

SUZI HAD COOLED OFF.

AND WE WERE ALL EXCITED TO SHOW OFF OUR HANDIWORK.

YOU'RE A **WONDER,** DAWN!

I HOPE YOU'LL COME BACK.

ANY TIME.

IF I HAD ONLY KNOWN HOW OFTEN "ANY TIME" WAS GOING TO BE, I MIGHT NOT HAVE SPOKEN SO QUICKLY.

CHAPTER 5

THE FIRST TIME I MET MARY ANNE, SHE WAS SITTING AT A CAFETERIA TABLE ALL BY HERSELF. THE BABY-SITTERS CLUB HAD JUST HAD A HUGE FIGHT.

THEY WERE ALL SITTING WITH OTHER FRIENDS -- EXCEPT FOR MARY ANNE.

THAT'S WHERE I CAME IN.

NOW THAT SHE AND KRISTY ARE FRIENDS AGAIN...

THEY'VE GONE BACK TO SITTING AT THEIR USUAL TABLE WITH THE SHILLABER TWINS.

45

HEY, GUYS.

SO??

ANY UPDATES?

MY DAD AND DAWN'S MOM WENT OUT ON *TWO* MORE DATES THIS WEEKEND.

THEY **DID?!**

WHERE'D THEY GO?

OUT TO DINNER AND THE MOVIES ON SATURDAY NIGHT...

AND THEN TO BRUNCH THE VERY NEXT MORNING.

EEEEEE!

YOU KNOW, IF YOUR PARENTS GET MARRIED...

SUDDENLY,
I KNEW.

48

KRISTY DIDN'T DISLIKE ME.

...AND THEY'LL GET MARRIED AND HAVE A BIG, BEAUTIFUL WEDDING, WITH TONS OF FLOWERS...

AND A *HUUUGE* CAKE!

SHE WAS JUST AFRAID OF BEING LEFT OUT.

HEY, UM, KRISTY.

AREN'T YOUR MOM AND WATSON PLANNING TO GET MARRIED SOON?

OOOOH, A REAL **MANSION**?

A REAL MANSION.

IT'S **HUGE**.

DO YOU GET TO REDECORATE YOUR ROOM? LIKE, HOWEVER YOU WANT?

I GUESS. BUT WHAT I REALLY WANT IS EXACTLY WHAT'S IN MY ROOM RIGHT NOW.

WHAAAAT? YOU'VE HAD THAT FOR **YEARS**.

JUST THINK! YOU COULD PROBABLY DO ANYTHING YOU WANTED TO YOUR NEW ROOM.

SPORTS THEMED...

YOUR FAVORITE COLORS...

OR EVEN SOMETHING HIGH TECH --

WHAT I **WANT** IS WHAT I'VE GOT.

SO LAY OFF, OKAY?

OKAY!

SEE YOU GUYS LATER.

LATER.

9:00 – Breakfast.

9:30 – Clean table.

10:00 – Kids get dressed.

10:30 – Straighten bedrooms.

11:00 – Still straightening rooms.

11:30 – Snacks for picnic??

AHA!

Brownie Mix

"Just Like M

12:00 – ~~Playtime~~ Clean kitchen.

pomf

flour

12:30 – Brownies!

12:50 – Head over to picnic!

STACEY.
PSSSST.
STACEY.

DAWN! YOU MADE IT!

UH...ARE YOU OKAY?

HOW MANY PIKE KIDS ARE THERE?

EIGHT. YOU KNOW THAT.

RIGHT, AND THERE ARE THREE BARRETT KIDS.

AND YOU AND ME AND CLAUDIA.

SO... FOURTEEN.

NOW COUNT THE PEOPLE IN THE BACKYARD.

BZZZZZZ.

HEY!

CLAUDIA! JORDAN GAVE ME THE BIZZER SIGN!

OH NO.

WHAT?

THE PIKE KIDS MADE IT UP. IT'S LIKE... AN INSULT OR SOMETHING?

JUST IGNORE HIM.

BUT HE GAVE ME THE BIZZER SIGN!

BZZZZZZZZZZZZ.

BIZZERS DON'T GET BROWNIES!!

THAT WAS A CLOSE ONE.

HEY, MARNIE. YOU WANT A BROWNIE?

STOP!!

WHAT ARE YOU DOING?!

WHAT ARE YOU DOING?!

MARNIE'S ALLERGIC.

SHE CAN'T EAT CHOCOLATE. IT MAKES HER REALLY SICK.

WHAT...? BUT...

MRS. BARRETT NEVER TOLD ME THAT.

Wednesday, May 27th

This evning I babysat for Dawn Shafers brother Jeff. I could tell he thoght he was to old for a baby-sitter but Dawn was sitting at the Barretts and her mom had suddenly gotten tickits to a concert and Mrs. Shaffer didnt want to leave Jeff alone at night. She called me at the last minute and luckly I was free. Sitting for Jeff was an easy job.

But! Dawn I noticed this is the second night in a row you've sat at the Barretts. And I looked in our apontment book and you were their four times last week. Maybe you are over doing it?

I am telling you this as a freind.

* claudia *

CHAPTER 7

SORRY! GOTTA GO! BARRETTS!

CLAUDIA WAS RIGHT.

WITH MRS. BARRETT'S DIVORCE AND JOB HUNT, IT SEEMED LIKE SHE ALWAYS NEEDED SOMEONE TO LOOK AFTER THE KIDS...

AND THEY LIKED ME BEST.

ONE TIME, I EVEN MISSED A MEETING OF THE BABY-SITTERS CLUB.

MRS. BARRETT HAD PROMISED SHE'D BE BACK BY 5:30, BUT ENDED UP STAYING OUT UNTIL 6 WITHOUT SO MUCH AS A CALL!

BUT I DID FINALLY GET UP THE NERVE TO TALK TO HER.

THANK YOU, DAWN. I DON'T KNOW WHAT I'D DO --

MRS. BARRETT?

HOW COME YOU DIDN'T TELL ME MARNIE'S ALLERGIC TO CHOCOLATE?

I...DIDN'T TELL YOU?

NO.

I ALMOST GAVE HER A PIECE OF BROWNIE THE OTHER DAY. MALLORY STOPPED ME JUST IN TIME.

MY GOODNESS!

DO THE KIDS HAVE ANY OTHER ALLERGIES?

NONE THAT WE'RE AWARE OF.

IS THERE ANYTHING ELSE I SHOULD KNOW?

JUST ONE THING. IF MY EX-HUSBAND EVER CALLS...

DON'T LET HIM **TALK** TO THE CHILDREN.

DON'T TELL HIM HE CAN **SEE** THE CHILDREN.

AND **DON'T** TELL HIM I'M OUT.

JUST SAY YOU'RE HELPING ME AND I'M BUSY. HE --

crash thnk

EEEEK!

SUZI!

KIDS...

I'LL TAKE CARE OF IT. WHY DON'T YOU DRY SUZI OFF?

BUDDY, GO GET THE PAPER TOWELS. WE'LL CLEAN UP.

AWWW.

THANK YOU AGAIN, DAWN. I HOPE YOU KNOW HOW MUCH WE APPRECIATE YOU.

WITH EVERYTHING THAT'S BEEN GOING ON, WELL, I JUST --

hug

ring

I'LL GET IT!

BUDDY! I TOLD YOU, YOU ARE NOT TO ANSWER THE -- !

DAD SAYS WHERE ARE WE?

YOU WERE S'POSED TO DROP OFF ME AND SUZI HALF AN HOUR AGO.

OH GRACIOUS, I COMPLETELY FORGOT!!

DAWN, I'LL SEE YOU WEDNESDAY!

SO THAT DIDN'T REALLY GO AS PLANNED.

IT'S BEEN A FEW WEEKS NOW, AND LIKE CLAUDIA SAID, I'VE BEEN SITTING FOR THE BARRETTS A **LOT**.

IT'S STARTING TO FEEL LIKE I'M, I DON'T KNOW, A STAND-IN MOM.

BUDDY? WHAT'S THE MATTER?

sniffle

M-MY HOMEWORK.

WELL, CAN I HELP? I'M PRETTY SMART.

I NEED **MOM'S** HELP.

THAT WASN'T THE WORST I HAD TO DEAL WITH, THOUGH.

URGHHHHHHH.

HWORKKK

AH!

WHERE IS IT, WHERE IS IT...

milk
butter
appt. 307

Emergency-
cell #
62-3015

5:30
up kids

HELLO?

MALLORY! THANK YOU SO MUCH FOR COMING.

SUZI'S BEEN THROWING UP AND I CAN'T GET AHOLD OF MRS. BARRETT. COULD YOU...?

I'M ON IT.

I SPENT THE REST OF THE DAY READING TO SUZI IN THE BATHROOM...

WHILE MALLORY TOOK CARE OF MARNIE AND BUDDY.

beep toktoktok

WHAT'S GOTTEN INTO YOU?

BOTH MY FAMILY AND MALLORY'S ENDED UP CATCHING THAT BUG.

CHAPTER 8

I WAS GLAD I COULD HELP, BUT BUDDY'S MOM SHOULD HAVE BEEN THE ONE HELPING HIM WITH HIS FAMILY TREE...

ding dong

sigh

BEING PROUD OF THE GOLD STAR...

HELLO, DAWN.

COME ON UPSTAIRS.

AND GETTING THE HUG.

THANKS, JANINE.

MARNIE WOULD HAVE BEEN IN SERIOUS TROUBLE IF MAL HADN'T BEEN AT THE PICNIC.

GOOD JOB, MALLORY!

AND SHE WAS REALLY HELPFUL WHEN SUZI GOT SICK.

TH-THANKS.

AND YOU KNOW...

I DIDN'T HAVE TO PASS YOUR CRAZY TEST TO DO IT.

HOLD ON JUST A --

ACTUALLY, YOU'RE RIGHT.

WE DID HAVE TO DO AN AWFUL LOT OF RESEARCH OURSELVES TO PUT THAT TOGETHER.

AND I **STILL** COULDN'T REMEMBER EVERYTHING.

WELL...

YOU GUYS MAKE A GOOD POINT.

AND MALLORY **HAS** BEEN REALLY HELPFUL, EVEN BEFORE WE INVITED HER TO JOIN THE CLUB.

rustle

IN THAT CASE...

HOW ABOUT A TASTY TOAST FOR OUR **NEW** JUNIOR MEMBER?

TO MALLORY!

THE REST OF THE MEETING WAS PRETTY NORMAL, UNTIL...

OH, BEFORE I FORGET...

KRISTY, I WANTED TO ASK YOU ABOUT SOMETHING.

WHAT?

I WAS BABY-SITTING FOR DAVID MICHAEL THE OTHER DAY...

YEAH, I REMEMBER.

UM... STACEY?

Pant pant

WHEN YOU MOVED, DID THEY PACK UP **EVERYTHING** IN THE VAN?

OH, OF COURSE. EVERY LAST THING.

THEY DIDN'T LEAVE **ANYTHING** BEHIND.

E-EVEN YOUR PETS??

???

Snuffle

OH, DAVID MICHAEL!

THEY WON'T PUT **LOUIE** IN THE VAN.

hahahaha

DAVID MICHAEL!

BUT TALKING TO HIM GOT ME THINKING.

WHAT ARE WE GOING TO DO ABOUT THE CLUB WHEN YOU MOVE?

IT'S ONLY A FEW MILES AWAY --

MOM WON'T LET ME BIKE HERE FROM WATSON'S.

COULD WE MEET SOMEWHERE ELSE?

BUT WE'D NEED A PHONE.

OUR CLIENTS HAVE TO KNOW WHERE TO REACH US.

STUPID, STUPID WATSON.

HEY, DON'T GET DOWN ON WATSON. IT'S NOT HIS FAULT.

IT'S NOT ANYBODY'S FAULT.

A LOT **YOU** KNOW.

I MAY KNOW MORE THAN YOU THINK.

YOU'RE NOT THE ONLY ONE WHOSE PARENTS GOT DIVORCED.

NO, BUT I'M THE ONLY ONE WHOSE MOM CHOSE TO GET MARRIED TO A GUY WHO'S SO RICH HE LIVES OVER ON **MILLIONAIRE'S LANE.**

AND **I'M** THE ONLY ONE WHO MAY HAVE TO DROP OUT OF THE CLUB. THE CLUB **I** STARTED.

KRISTY!

WE COULDN'T RUN THE CLUB WITHOUT YOU. IT WOULDN'T BE RIGHT.

CHAPTER 9

THE FATE OF THE CLUB WAS HANGING IN THE AIR -- MUCH LIKE THE WINTER CHILL THAT JUST WOULDN'T GO AWAY.

BUT IT WAS MEMORIAL DAY WEEKEND, AND MOM WAS DETERMINED TO HOST A PICNIC.

MOM, THIS MIGHT BE THE FIRST PICNIC EVER ATTENDED BY PEOPLE IN DOWN JACKETS.

FOR PITY'S SAKE, DAWN. IT'S LOVELY OUT.

INCOMING!

ACK!

SPlsh.

OF COURSE, MOST PEOPLE ALREADY HAD PLANS. IN THE END, THE ONLY ONES WHO COULD MAKE IT WERE MY GRANDPARENTS, THE SPIERS, THE BARRETTS...

DO YOU THINK I COULD SUBSTITUTE RAW HONEY FOR SUGAR?

UM...

AND KRISTY AND DAVID MICHAEL.

WHAT IF, INSTEAD OF TRYING TO MAKE ALL THIS FANCY STUFF, WE JUST DO HAMBURGERS, HOT DOGS, AND POTATO SALAD?

HOT DOGS! DO YOU EVEN KNOW WHAT'S IN A --

WE'RE IN CONNECTICUT NOW, MOM.

PEOPLE **BARBECUE** THINGS HERE. WE SHOULD TRY TO SERVE FOOD THEY'LL EAT.

SOON...

KEEP AN EYE ON THEM. THIS IS A GOOD CHANCE TO SEE HOW THEY'RE DOING.

AND WHETHER OR NOT YOUR GRANDPARENTS STILL DISAPPROVE OF MY DAD.

WE MIGHT HAVE TO AVERT A **CRISIS.**

HEY...

I'M GLAD EVERYTHING TURNED OUT OKAY.

YEAH.

YOUR PARENTS REALLY LIKE EACH OTHER.

YOU MIGHT ACTUALLY END UP BEING SISTERS.

KRISTY...

ARE YOU ALL RIGHT?

I...

WELL, YOU KNOW.

MY MOM GETTING MARRIED, AND THE MOVE AND ALL. IT'S A LOT.

I'M GOING TO BE SO FAR AWAY FROM YOU GUYS, AND I DON'T KNOW WHAT'S HAPPENING WITH THE CLUB...

sniffle

YOU DON'T WANT TO BE LEFT BEHIND.

WHEN WE MOVED HERE, WE HAD TO LEAVE A LOT BEHIND.

OUR HOUSE, OUR COUSINS AND BEST FRIENDS, DAD...

THEY'RE ALL THOUSANDS OF MILES AWAY NOW.

BUT WE STILL TALK ALL THE TIME.

YOU'RE ONLY MOVING ACROSS TOWN. DO YOU REALLY THINK WE'RE GOING TO LET OUR FRIENDSHIP CHANGE OVER A FEW MILES?

Tuesday, June 2

This afternoon I baby-sat for Buddy, Suzi, and Marnie Barrett. What a time I had! I don't know if it's the weather or problems with the divorce or what, but the kids were wild. Wild and cranky. I'm sure the sitter they really wanted was Dawn. I don't know how you handle them, Dawn. I hope they behave better for you than they do for me.

By the way, there was a really strange phone call from Mr. Barrett today, wanting to know where Buddy was. I wouldn't give him any information. When I told Mrs. Barrett about the call, she turned purple (not really) and said he shouldn't have called when he knew darn well she'd be out. What's going on?

I think we should all be careful of calls from Mr. Barrett.

Mary Anne

TODAY, FOR THE FIRST TIME IN AGES, I WASN'T THE ONE BABY-SITTING FOR THE BARRETTS.

I DIDN'T ENVY MARY ANNE -- IT HAD BEEN RAINING FOR THREE DAYS STRAIGHT.

PEW!

PEW!

I GOT YOU! YOU'RE DEAD!

WELL, I'M NOT DEAD FOR LONG, BECAUSE I'M COMING INTO YOUR HOUSE.

STAND ASIDE, MARTIAN MAN.

MARTIAN?! I'M A COWBOY! FROM **VENUS**!

THIS IS OBVIOUSLY A **VENUS** WEAPON!

DAWN?

ALL RIGHT, WHO WANTS TO --

BIZZ

BUDDY, YOU GIVE ONE MORE BIZZER SIGN TO ANYONE TODAY -- **ANYONE** -- AND YOU'LL HAVE TO STAY IN YOUR ROOM UNTIL YOUR MOTHER COMES HOME.

WILL **NOT.**

YES, YOU WILL. I'M IN CHARGE HERE, AND WHAT I SAY GOES.

WILL YOU TELL MOM IF I'M BAD?

I MIGHT.

TATTLETALE!

THAT'S THE WAY IT IS.

NOW. YOU KNOW WHAT WE'RE GOING TO DO TODAY?

NOT READ.

NOT COLOR.

NOT WATCH TV.

NOT PLAY *CANDY LAND.*

NOPE. I CAN TELL YOU'RE TIRED OF THE SAME OLD RAINY-DAY STUFF.

SO TODAY WE'RE GOING TO GO OUTSIDE FOR A **PUDDLE WALK.**

JUMP IN AS MANY PUDDLES AS YOU CAN.

TRY TO MAKE BIG SPLASHES!

aaaaAAAA

AAAACK!

SPLOOSH

HE **SPLASHED** ME!

GOOD!

YOU'RE WEARING YOUR SWIMSUIT AND RAINCOAT.

THESE CLOTHES ARE **SUPPOSED** TO GET WET.

OHHHHHHHH.

tmp tmp

giggle

OKAY, LET'S JUST LEAVE OUR FLIP-FLOPS BY THE --

ring ring ri

SPACE PHONE!

HOLD ON!

NOOOOO! VENUS **NEEDS** ME!

HELLO, BARRETT RESIDENCE.

BZZZZZZ

BUDDY! I TOLD YOU WHAT WOULD HAPPEN IF YOU DID THAT AGAIN.

GO TO YOUR ROOM.

SORRY ABOUT THAT. HELLO?

HELLO? WHO'S THIS?

stomp

STOMP

THIS IS MARY ANNE SPIER, THE SITTER. WHO'S THIS?

THIS IS MR. BARRETT.

WOULD YOU MIND PUTTING BUDDY ON?

OR SUZI?

I'M SORRY, THEY'RE...AT A FRIEND'S HOUSE.

OH, **FINE.**

Slam

beep beep beep

WHEN MRS. BARRETT GOT HOME, THERE WAS QUITE THE SCENE.

BUDDY WAS MAD BECAUSE HE'D BEEN PUNISHED...

MRS. BARRETT WAS MAD BECAUSE BUDDY HAD MISBEHAVED...

AND SHE WAS **VERY** UPSET THAT MR. BARRETT HAD CALLED.

HE'S ONLY SUPPOSED TO SPEAK TO THE KIDS ON ALTERNATING TUESDAYS, AND THIS IS THE WRONG DAY.

IT'S PART OF THE CUSTODY ARRANGEMENT, AND HE CAN'T KEEP HIS OWN **SCHEDULE** STRAIGHT!

AND BUDDY, WHAT IS THE **MATTER** WITH YOU?

I GET NOTES FROM YOUR TEACHER, YOU GIVE MARY ANNE TROUBLE...

I DON'T HAVE **TIME** FOR THIS, YOUNG MAN.

I CANNOT BE YOUR MOTHER AND FATHER, RUN THIS HOUSEHOLD, LOOK FOR A JOB...

AND STRAIGHTEN OUT THE MESSES YOU GET YOURSELF INTO.

IT'S TOO MUCH TO ASK OF ANYBODY.

CHAPTER 11

THE RAIN DIDN'T LET UP AFTER THAT.

Lptptptptp

I DIDN'T REALLY MIND. IT MADE ME THINK OF THE RAINY SEASON IN CALIFORNIA.

PLUS, MY MOM WAS IN A GREAT MOOD.

SHE AND MR. SPIER WERE TALKING ON THE PHONE ALMOST EVERY NIGHT.

AND I HADN'T HAD TO TELL HER TO FIX HER EARRINGS IN **THREE DAYS STRAIGHT** -- A NEW RECORD.

TOO BAD THE BARRETT KIDS WEREN'T NEARLY AS HIGH-SPIRITED.

HOW ABOUT... PUTTING ON A PLAY?

NOOOOOOO.

MAKING OUR OWN COMIC BOOK?

TOO HARD.

WELL, WHAT DO **YOU** WANT TO DO?

I DUNNOOOOOO.

sigh.

HEY!

THE RAIN STOPPED!

LET'S GO **OUTSIDE!**

WAIT!

HOLD ON A SEC. WE'VE GOTTA BE SMART.

BUDDY, YOU'RE READY AS SOON AS YOU PUT ON YOUR BOOTS.

SO YOU CAN GO AHEAD.

BUT, SUZI AND MARNIE, IT'S CHILLY OUT TODAY. WE HAVE TO GET YOU BUNDLED UP FIRST.

NO FAIR!!

IT'LL ONLY BE A MINUTE. BUDDY, BOOTS AND JACKET.

OKAYYYY!

grumble

HEY, DAWN. HEY, MOM.

THE DOOR WAS OPEN.

I GOT YOUR NOTE AND CAME OVER LIKE YOU SAID TO. WHAT'S GOING ON?

HONEY, BUDDY'S MISSING. EVERYONE'S OUT LOOKING. HAVE YOU SEEN HIM?

SURE I HAVE. AND HE'S NOT MISSING.

WHAT? WHERE IS HE??

HE'S AT HIS LESSON.

HUH?

SUZI, DOES BUDDY TAKE ANY KIND OF LESSONS? LIKE PIANO OR ART?

UH...

NO...?

HONEY, WHAT MAKES YOU THINK BUDDY IS AT A LESSON?

WELL...

AT THE SAME TIME MRS. KATZ AND SANDY PICKED ME UP FOR MY PIANO LESSON...

I SAW SOMEONE PICK BUDDY UP.

SO I THOUGHT...

CHAPTER 12

DO YOU REMEMBER ANYTHING ELSE ABOUT THE CAR?

um...

DID YOU SEE THE LICENSE PLATE? THE DRIVER?

I DON'T...

WAS IT A MAN OR A WOMAN?

I DON'T **KNOW**, OKAY?

WE LIVE THREE HOUSES AWAY, AND BESIDES, I WASN'T PAYING ATTENTION. I DIDN'T THINK THERE WAS ANY **REASON** TO.

MRS. KATZ PICKED ME UP, AND I SAW BUDDY GET INTO A CAR IN HIS DRIVEWAY. THAT'S **ALL**.

BUT YOU'RE SURE IT WAS A BLUE CAR.

YEAH.

A BLUE CAR.

AND YOU DIDN'T NOTICE THE DRIVER.

NO.

DID BUDDY LOOK SCARED AS HE GOT IN THE CAR? LIKE HE DIDN'T WANT TO GO?

NO. HE WAS OPENING THE DOOR AND GETTING IN.

DID YOU RECOGNIZE THE CAR? HAVE YOU SEEN IT AROUND HERE BEFORE?

I...

I DON'T KNOW. IT WAS JUST A CAR.

ANY MORE QUESTIONS?

JUST A COUPLE.

JORDAN, I KNOW WE'VE ASKED YOU THIS BEFORE.

BUT ARE YOU **POSITIVE** YOU DIDN'T SEE THE DRIVER? NOT EVEN WHETHER IT WAS A MAN OR A WOMAN?

I WAS LOOKING AT BUDDY, NOT THE DRIVER.

ONE LAST THING.

ABOUT WHAT TIME DID YOU SEE BUDDY GET INTO THE CAR?

MOM, WHAT TIME DID MRS. KATZ PICK ME UP?

11:15, HONEY.

11:15, THEN. MY PIANO LESSON WAS AT 11:30.

scribble

AS FOR ME, THE POLICE MOSTLY HAD QUESTIONS ABOUT MR. BARRETT.

THEY SEEMED DISAPPOINTED WHEN I SAID I DIDN'T KNOW MUCH ABOUT HIM, OR HIS DIVORCE WITH MRS. BARRETT...

BUT THEY WERE **VERY** INTERESTED WHEN THEY FOUND OUT THAT MRS. BARRETT DIDN'T WANT MR. BARRETT CALLING THE KIDS.

DAWN?

MARNIE WILL BE AWAKE SOON.

I SHOULD GET BACK TO WORK.

YOU'RE A BRAVE GIRL. I'M VERY PROUD OF YOU.

SHOULD'VE SEEN ME BEFORE YOU GOT HERE.

WELL, JEFF AND I WILL BE HELPING WITH THE NEIGHBORHOOD SEARCH, SO...

JUST YELL IF YOU NEED ANYTHING.

THANKS, MOM.

FOR THE NEXT HOUR, THE POLICE CAME AND WENT.

THEY SEARCHED THE HOUSE FOR AN ADDRESS BOOK OR ANY CLUE AS TO WHERE MR. BARRETT MIGHT BE, BUT DIDN'T FIND MUCH.

MALLORY VOLUNTEERED TO LOOK AFTER SUZI AT THE PIKES' HOUSE, AND I CALLED TO SEE IF SUZI REMEMBERED WHERE HER DAD LIVED.

UM...IN HIS 'PARTMENT?

WHILE ALL OF THIS WAS GOING ON, I STILL HAD MARNIE TO LOOK AFTER.

ring
ring
ring

SO YOU'RE TELLING ME THAT MY EX-HUSBAND... **TOOK**...BUDDY THIS MORNING.

AND YOU DIDN'T KNOW UNTIL **BUDDY** CALLED?

THAT'S CORRECT. I DON'T MEAN TO ALARM YOU...

BUT HAS YOUR DIVORCE BEEN A FRIENDLY ONE?

NO, IT HASN'T. WHY?

BECAUSE, WELL, A LOT OF MISSING KIDS ARE CHILDREN OF DIVORCE.

THEY'VE BEEN TAKEN BY PARENTS WHO WANT CUSTODY, BUT HAVEN'T BEEN GRANTED IT.

OH, **NO.** HAM AND I HAVE PROBLEMS, BUT HE'D NEVER **KIDNAP** THE KIDS. I MEAN, HE ALREADY GETS THEM TWICE A...

TWICE A...

scoot

OOPS.

132

Slam
tptptp
thud

DAWN!

BUDDY!

I'M SORRY I MADE YOU WORRY.

I'M **STARVING.** DO WE HAVE COOKIES?

LET'S SEE WHAT WE CAN FIND.

133

WHILE BUDDY AND I WENT ON OUR LITTLE MISSION, THE POLICE GOT THE FULL STORY OUT OF MR. BARRETT.

MRS. BARRETT HAD BEEN MIXING UP THEIR SCHEDULE A LOT, AND WHEN HE REALIZED THAT SHE HAD CONFUSED THE DATES AGAIN TODAY, HE GOT MAD.

HE DECIDED TO TEACH HER A LESSON.

HIS PLAN WAS TO COME BY, TAKE THE KIDS, AND WAIT FOR MRS. BARRETT TO FIGURE OUT HER MISTAKE.

WHEN HE SAW BUDDY ALL BY HIMSELF, HE THOUGHT IT'D BE EASIEST TO JUST TAKE HIM.

HAM83

THEY WENT TO LUNCH AND A THEME PARK, BUT BUDDY DIDN'T SEEM HAPPY.

WHEN MR. BARRETT ASKED WHAT WAS WRONG, BUDDY SAID HE WAS WORRIED ABOUT **ME**, BECAUSE I DIDN'T KNOW WHERE HE WAS.

THAT WAS WHEN MR. BARRETT REALIZED THAT HIS EX-WIFE WASN'T EVEN HOME.

AND WHO KNEW WHAT A BABY-SITTER WOULD DO WHEN SHE FOUND OUT ONE OF HER CHARGES WAS MISSING?

THE POLICE GAVE MR. BARRETT A WARNING, BUT THAT WAS IT.

THEY DID STRONGLY SUGGEST, HOWEVER, THAT THE BARRETTS TALK TO THEIR LAWYERS ABOUT THEIR CUSTODY ARRANGEMENTS.

BUT THAT WASN'T QUITE THE END OF IT.

I HAD SOMETHING TO TELL MRS. BARRETT.

135

CHAPTER 13

I WENT OVER THE NEXT MORNING.

MRS. BARRETT HAD SUGGESTED THAT MR. BARRETT TAKE THE KIDS FOR THE DAY, AND I'D NEVER HEARD THE HOUSE SO QUIET.

IT WAS WEIRD.

SO, DAWN, WHAT IS IT YOU WANTED TO TALK ABOUT?

WELL...

I REALLY LIKE BUDDY, MARNIE, AND SUZI, BUT...

I CAN'T BABY-SIT FOR THEM ANYMORE.

YOU **CAN'T?** IT'S NOT BECAUSE OF WHAT HAPPENED YESTERDAY, IS IT?

um...

WE'RE GOING TO STRAIGHTEN OUR PROBLEMS OUT, DAWN.

WE'RE GOING TO TALK TO OUR LAWYERS, AND MAYBE A COUNSELOR, TOO.

YOU WON'T HAVE ANY MORE ISSUES WITH MY EX-HUSBAND.

THAT'S NOT REALLY...

THE PROBLEM IS, UH...

I'VE HAD A LOT OF TROUBLE BECAUSE OF...

BECAUSE OF MISTAKES YOU'VE MADE.

SO I'LL BE SITTING FOR THEM THREE MORE TIMES.

I THINK IT WAS VERY BRAVE OF YOU TO HAVE THE TALK IN THE FIRST PLACE.

YEAH. YOU CAME TO A REASONABLE COMPROMISE.

HOW ARE THE KIDS DOING NOW, ANYWAY? SINCE THE INCIDENT?

THEY'RE GOOD, I THINK. MARNIE'S TOO LITTLE TO REMEMBER...

MALLORY TOOK GREAT CARE OF SUZI WHILE THINGS WERE GOING DOWN...

AND BUDDY'S OKAY.

HE'S CONFUSED, BUT HIS PARENTS EXPLAINED THAT THEY HAVE SOME PROBLEMS THEY'RE WORKING ON.

THE IDEA OF PARENTS KIDNAPPING THEIR OWN CHILDREN IS SCARY.

YEAH.

WHEW.

click

WE DISCUSSED BUSINESS FOR A FEW MINUTES...

AND THEN...

ahem

I'VE BEEN THINKING ABOUT WHAT TO DO WITH THE CLUB AFTER I MOVE.

I MEAN, I KNOW WE HAVE ALL SUMMER BEFORE THAT HAPPENS, BUT I CAN'T HELP WORRYING ABOUT IT.

SO I'VE COME TO A DECISION.

MY DECISION...

IS TO RAISE OUR CLUB DUES.

WHAT?

THE ONLY SOLUTION I CAN THINK OF IS TO PAY SOMEONE TO DRIVE ME TO AND FROM CLUB MEETINGS. NOT A CAB DRIVER, BUT SOMEONE WHO'D LIKE TO EARN A LITTLE EXTRA MONEY.

SOMEONE YOUNG WHO'S JUST LEARNED TO DRIVE --

CHARLIE!

CHARLIE WILL BE ABLE TO DRIVE THEN, WON'T HE?

KRISTY, THAT'S A GREAT IDEA!

AND I BET HE'LL BE **DYING** FOR EXCUSES TO USE THE CAR.

BUT...DO YOU MIND PAYING FOR IT OUT OF OUR DUES?

I KNOW IT'S KIND OF --

KRISTY, YOU'RE THE **PRESIDENT.**

IT'S THE PERFECT SOLUTION.

NO KRISTY...

NO CLUB.

ANN M. MARTIN'S The Baby-sitters Club is one of the most popular series in the history of publishing — with more than 176 million books in print worldwide — and inspired a generation of young readers. Her novels include *Belle Teal*, *A Corner of the Universe* (a Newbery Honor book), *Here Today*, *A Dog's Life*, and *On Christmas Eve*, as well as the much-loved collaborations, *P.S. Longer Letter Later* and *Snail Mail No More*, with Paula Danziger, and *The Doll People* and *The Meanest Doll in the World*, written with Laura Godwin and illustrated by Brian Selznick. She lives in upstate New York.

GALE GALLIGAN is a graduate of NYU and the Savannah College of Art and Design. Her comics have appeared in a number of anthologies, and she worked as a production assistant on *Drama* by Raina Telgemeier. Gale lives in Pleasantville, New York. Visit her online at www.galesaur.com.

DON'T MISS THE OTHER
BABY-SITTERS CLUB GRAPHIC NOVELS!